Date: 5/23/12

THE Best OF THE Best

BLAZERS

Skateboarding GREATS

BY LORI POLYDOROS

Reading Consultant:
Barbara J. Fox
Reading Specialist
North Carolina State University

CAPSTONE PRESS
a capstone imprint

Blazers is published by Capstone Press,
151 Good Counsel Drive, P.O. Box 669, Mankato, Minnesota 56002.
www.capstonepub.com

 Books published by Capstone Press are manufactured with paper
containing at least 10 percent post-consumer waste.

Library of Congress Cataloging-in-Publication Data
Polydoros, Lori, 1968–
    Skateboarding greats / by Lori Polydoros.
    p. cm.—(Blazers. Best of the best)
    Includes bibliographical references and index.
    Summary: "Lists and describes the top skateboarders of the past and today"—Provided by
publisher.
    ISBN 978-1-4296-6498-1 (library binding)
    ISBN 978-1-4296-7253-5 (paperback)
    1. Skateboarders—Biography—Juvenile literature. I. Title.
GV859.812.P65 2012
796.220922—dc22
[B]   2011002476

Editorial Credits
Mandy Robbins, editor; Kyle Grenz, designer; Eric Manske, production specialist

Photo Credits
AP Images: Jae C. Hong, cover (bottom), Lori Shepler, cover (top): Chad Santos, 24;
CORBIS: NewSport/Steve Boyle, 1(bottom); Don Walhein, 11; Getty Images Inc.: AFP/
Robyn Beck, 12, Blixah/Michael Burnett, 16-17, Christian Petersen, 18-19, Harry How, 8-9,
Jonathan Ferrey, 1(top), LatinContent/Gabriel Affonso Morales, 20-21, Robert Cianflone,
6-7, Stephen Dunn, 14-15, WireImage/J. Shearer, 27, WireImage/Phillip Ellsworth, 22-23;
Newscom: Icon SMI 558/Tony Donaldson, 28-29, ZUMA Press, 4-5

Artistic Effects
Shutterstock: Ashims, Nayashkova Olga, Pakhnyushcha, sabri deniz kizil

**The publisher does not endorse products whose logos may appear on objects in images
in this book.**

 WARNING: Do not attempt to ride a skateboard or perform skateboarding
tricks without the appropriate safety gear.

Printed in the United States of America in Stevens Point, Wisconsin.
032011   006111WZF11

TABLE OF CONTENTS

Higher AND Harder THAN Ever

Pro skateboarders catch big air and **grind** over rails and stairs. Skateboarding greats fly higher and flip harder than ever.

Skateboarding can be dangerous. Sometimes all that stands between a rider and a brain injury is a helmet.

TRICKED OUT!

GRIND
to ride on top of a metal obstacle; named after the sound the skateboard makes when it rubs against the metal

5

Tony Hawk has won 73 out of 103 competitions. After 12 tries, Tony pulled off a **900** at the X Games in 1999. It didn't count for the competition, but he was the first skater to ever do it.

FACT Tony has created more than 80 tricks.

Tony Hawk
(1968-)

TRICKED OUT!

900
two-and-a-half rotations
on a skateboard in midair

Ryan Sheckler
(1989-)

In 2003 Ryan Sheckler was the only skater to land every trick at the X Games. Ryan won the U.S. Skateboarding Championship three years in a row.

FACT In 2004 Ryan became the youngest skater to win an X Games gold medal. He was 15 years old.

Rodney Mullen
(1966-)

Rodney Mullen invented most of the **street ollie** and flip tricks in the 1980s. Mullen's moves form the basis of **vert** and street skating today.

street–a style of skateboarding involving tricks on sidewalk and street obstacles like benches or railings

vert–a skating style performed on vertical ramps

OLLIE
a skater steps on the board's tail to make the board rise into the air

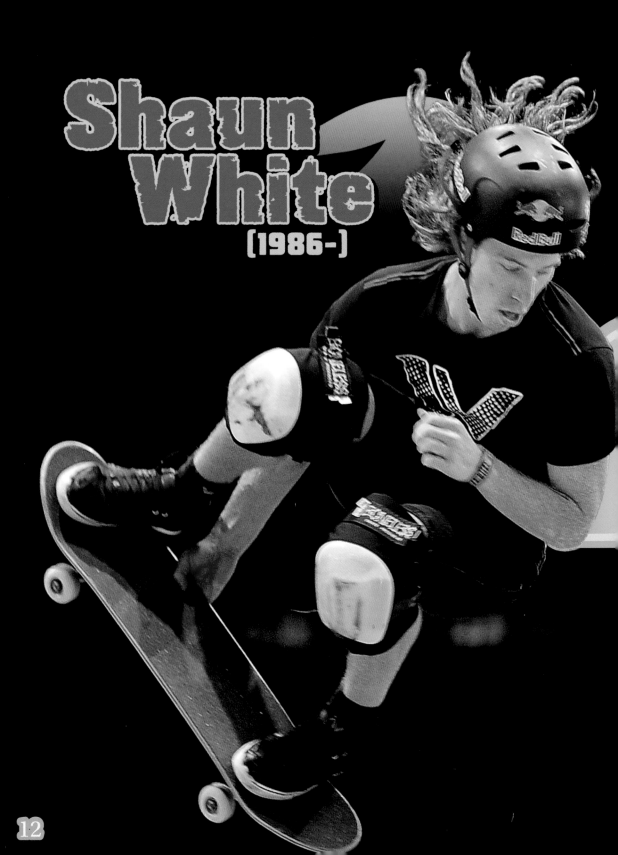

Shaun White

(1986-)

 Shaun was the first athlete to win medals in the Summer and Winter X Games in two different sports.

Shaun White takes vert riding to another level. He's the only skater to pull off his insane Double McTwist 1260. Shaun also uses his skills as a professional snowboarder.

 **DOUBLE MCTWIST 1260** a skater front flips twice, spinning out of each flip, and then completes three-and-a-half spins

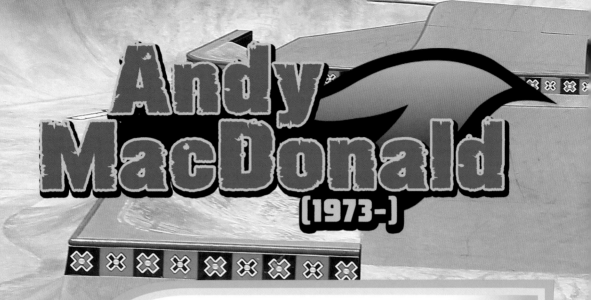

Andy MacDonald

(1973-)

Andy MacDonald rides vert, park, mega ramp, and more. He was the World Cup Champion eight years in a row. Andy has also competed in every X Games since the event began in 1995.

park—a style of skateboarding involving tricks on bowls, ramps, walls, and other obstacles

mega ramp—a ramp used in skateboarding big air; the mega ramp is nine stories high and about as long as a football field

FACT Andy has earned 19 X Games medals.

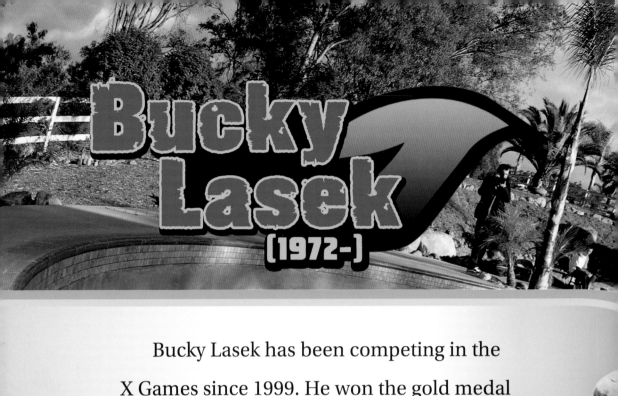

Bucky Lasek
(1972-)

Bucky Lasek has been competing in the X Games since 1999. He won the gold medal in X Games vert two years in a row—twice! No one has beaten Bucky's four vert wins.

FACT Bucky started skateboarding at age 12 after his bicycle was stolen.

Danny Way holds the records for the longest and the highest jumps on a skateboard. The longest jump was 79 feet (24 meters). The highest jump was 23.5 feet (7.2 m).

 Danny jumped over the Great Wall of China in 2005!

Danny Way
(1974–)

record–when something is done better
than anyone has ever done it before

Bob Burnquist

(1976-)

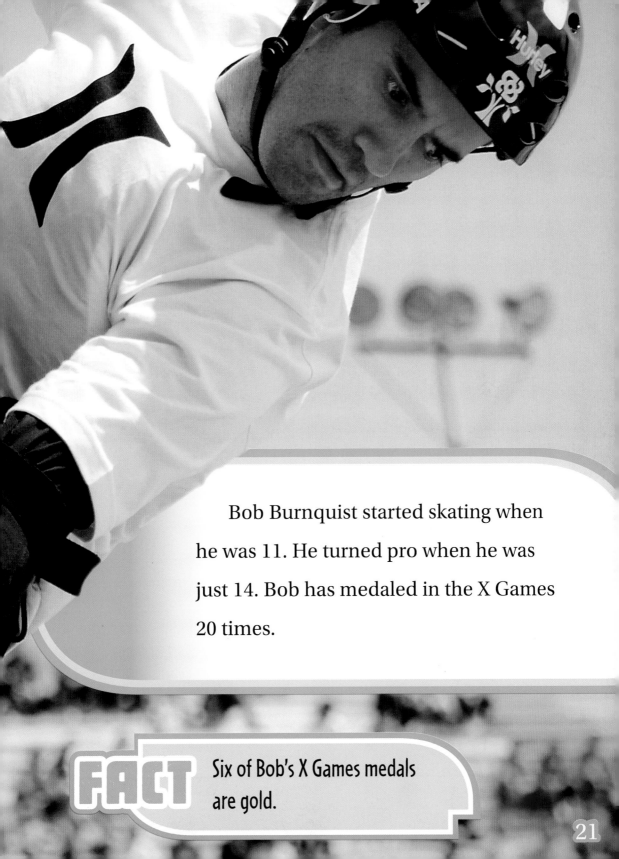

Bob Burnquist started skating when he was 11. He turned pro when he was just 14. Bob has medaled in the X Games 20 times.

FACT Six of Bob's X Games medals are gold.

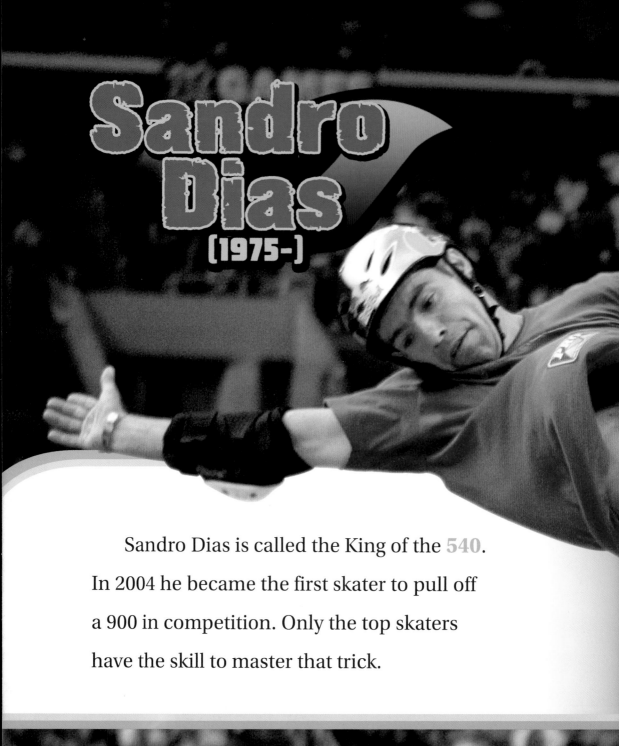

Sandro Dias

(1975-)

Sandro Dias is called the King of the **540**. In 2004 he became the first skater to pull off a 900 in competition. Only the top skaters have the skill to master that trick.

TRICKED OUT!

540
one-and-a-half rotations on a skateboard in midair

Daewon Song
(1975-)

Korean-American skater Daewon Song combines old and new tricks. He is famous for videos where he rides over obstacles. Daewon's skills make him one of the top street skaters of all time.

obstacle—an object such as a curb or a railing

Paul Rodriguez Jr.

(1984-)

Paul Rodriguez Jr. was named *TransWorld SKATEboarding* magazine's Rookie of the Year in 2002. In 2004 and 2005, Paul won gold medals in the X Games street skating competition.

 Paul won his first X Games gold medal in vert in 2009.

Elissa Steamer

(1975-)

Elissa Steamer has blazed a path for female skaters for 20 years. She has earned four X Games gold medals. Greats like Elissa keep skateboarding fans coming back for more.

FACT In 2003 and 2004, Elissa was voted the best female skater in the world by *Check It Out Girls Magazine*.

Glossary

mega ramp (MEG-uh RAMP)—a ramp used in skateboarding big air; the mega ramp is nine stories high and about as long as a football field

obstacle (OB-stuh-kuhl)—an object such as a curb or a railing; skaters perform tricks on obstacles

park (PARK)—a style of skateboarding involving tricks on bowls, ramps, walls, and other obstacles

record (REK-urd)—when something is done better than anyone has ever done it before

street (STREET)—a style of skateboarding involving tricks on sidewalk and street obstacles such as railings, benches, picnic tables, and steps

vert (VURT)—a skating style performed on vertical ramps such as halfpipes

X Games (EX GAYMS)—an annual sporting event that focuses on extreme sports

Read More

Fitzpatrick, Jim. *Tony Hawk.* The World's Greatest Athletes. Chanhassen, Minn.: Child's World, 2007.

Kjelle, Marylou Morano. *Extreme Skateboarding with Paul Rodriguez Jr.* Extreme Sports. Hockessin, Del.: Mitchell Lane Publishers, 2007.

Mattern, Joanne. *Skateboarding.* Action Sports. Vero Beach, Fla.: Rourke Publishing, 2009.

Internet Sites

FactHound offers a safe, fun way to find Internet sites related to this book. All of the sites on FactHound have been researched by our staff.

Here's all you do:

Visit *www.facthound.com*

Type in this code: 9781429664981

Super-cool stuff! Check out projects, games and lots more at **www.capstonekids.com**

Index